MW01378555

Capstone Short Biographies

Women in Earth Science Careers

by Jetty Kahn

Consultant:
Ellen P. Metzger
Professor of Geology
San Jose State University
San Jose, California

CAPSTONE
HIGH/LOW BOOKS
an imprint of Capstone Press
Mankato, Minnesota

Capstone High/Low Books are published by Capstone Press
818 North Willow Street • Mankato, Minnesota 56001
http://www.capstone-press.com

Printed in the United States of America.

Library of Congress Cataloging-in-Publication Data
Kahn, Jetty.
Women in earth science careers/by Jetty Kahn.
p. cm.—(Capstone short biographies)
Summary: Describes the careers of five women working in the earth sciences: Sheryl Luzzadder Beach, Sandra Corso, Jami Girard, Kelley Anne Gittis, and Patricia Rogers.
ISBN 0-7368-0012-3
1. Women earth scientists—United States—Biography—Juvenile literature. [1. Earth scientists. 2. Women—Biography.] I. Title. II. Series.
QE21.K34 1999
550´.92´273—dc21 98-18453
[B] CIP
AC

Editorial Credits
Colleen Sexton, editor; Timothy Halldin, cover designer; Sheri Gosewisch, photo researcher

Photo Credits
Images International/Erwin C. Nielsen, 4
Jami Girard, 24, 27, 28
Jet Propulsion Laboratory/California Institute of Technology, 43
Jim Wheeler, 10
Kelley Anne Gittis, 30, 33, 35, 36
NASA, 40
Patricia Rogers, 38
Rainbow/Dan McCoy, 7
Sandra Corso, 18, 20, 23
Shaffer Photography/James L. Shaffer, 8
Timothy Beach, cover, 12, 16
Visuals Unlimited/Mark E. Gibson, 15

Table of Contents

Chapter 1

Earth Science

Earth scientists study the parts of Earth. They study everything from the tops of mountains to the ocean floor. Some earth scientists study matter deep within Earth. Others study the atmosphere, space, or other planets. Their findings offer clues about how Earth formed.

Earth scientists work in many fields. For example, geologists study rocks. Some geologists study non-living matter in rocks called minerals. Some geologists study rocks to learn about the history of Earth.

Other types of earth scientists include hydrologists and geophysicists. Hydrologists

Some earth scientists study how mountains formed.

study water. Hydrologists may study oceans, rivers, lakes, or underground water supplies. Geophysicists study energy within Earth such as the force of volcanoes. Earth scientists in these fields and many others try to understand how the earth works.

Education

People who want to be earth scientists need to be curious about the world. Curiosity leads scientists to ask questions about the world and to work to find the answers.

The minimum requirement to be an earth scientist is a four-year college degree. Earth scientists need an education in science and math. At first, students learn about the broad topic of earth science. Later, students usually choose one area of earth science to study.

Earth science students also take computer classes. Computers are important tools for creating maps and charts. Computers also help earth scientists solve math problems that relate to their studies.

Some geophysicists study volcanoes.

Many earth scientists have master's degrees. Some study more and earn doctorates. A doctorate is the highest degree given by a university.

Earth Scientists at Work

Earth scientists work for many organizations. Some work for the government or in universities. Others work for companies or

Some earth scientists study floods and work to lessen the damage they cause.

environmental groups. The focus of earth scientists' jobs may depend on where they work.

Earth scientists who work for the government may manage natural resources. A natural resource is anything in nature that is useful to people. Earth scientists may make sure people have enough water and that the water is safe to drink. Other earth scientists who work for the government may study weather patterns and geological forces. These scientists try to figure out when natural disasters such as floods, earthquakes, and volcano eruptions will occur.

Earth scientists who work in universities usually teach. They also may perform research in their chosen fields. Researchers study a subject by doing experiments.

Businesses also hire earth scientists. These scientists may study places where people want to build roads or buildings. Earth scientists make sure the ground is safe. They also may study how roads and buildings will affect the surrounding area.

Some companies make products from natural resources. For example, mining companies dig up minerals for use in many products. Earth scientists help these companies find minerals.

Earth scientists who work for environmental groups try to protect Earth. These scientists may study places where people are harming the environment. They also may write articles or give speeches about their findings. These earth scientists show how people's actions affect Earth.

Chapter 2

Sheryl Luzzadder Beach

Sheryl Luzzadder Beach began learning about hydrology when she was 17 years old. She became interested in the study of water after floods struck her hometown of Red Bluff, California.

Beach studied geography in college. She learned about different climates and land features. She studied how these elements affect people. Beach earned a doctorate in geography from the University of Minnesota.

Today, Beach teaches geography at George Mason University in Fairfax, Virginia. She also conducts hydrology research in many areas of the world.

Sheryl Luzzadder Beach teaches geography and conducts research in hydrology.

Sheryl Luzzadder Beach studies groundwater.

Groundwater Studies

Beach studies groundwater. Most groundwater is close to the earth's surface. Groundwater forms when rain and melted snow seep into the earth. The water collects in spaces between rocks and sometimes flows like an underground river. People dig wells to reach groundwater. Wells provide water to homes, factories, and farms.

Beach studies the composition of groundwater. Groundwater picks up minerals from rocks as it moves. Minerals break down and become part of the groundwater. Beach tests groundwater. Water with too many minerals can harm people, animals, and crops.

Beach performed groundwater research in California and Nevada. The Alturas Valley in California receives twice as much rain each year as the Surprise Valley in Nevada. Large rivers flow across the Alturas Valley. The Surprise Valley has only a few small streams. This area is much drier than the Alturas Valley.

Beach compared the quality of the groundwater in the two areas. She expected the groundwater quality in the Alturas Valley to be better. The land there is wetter. She knew a greater amount of groundwater moves faster. Groundwater picks up fewer minerals if it moves faster. That makes the water quality better.

The groundwater quality in the Surprise Valley was as good as the groundwater quality in the Alturas Valley. Beach conducted a study to find out why. She discovered that farmers in the Surprise Valley pump large quantities of groundwater to water their crops. The farmers pumped 12 times as much groundwater as farmers did in the wetter Alturas Valley. This meant that the groundwater was being drawn quickly through the ground. The water picked up few minerals.

Making Maps

Beach creates groundwater maps on a computer. The maps show how groundwater flows in certain areas. Groundwater follows the slope of the land. Beach must carefully study land features to create good groundwater maps. She also tests groundwater in different places and records its mineral content on the map.

Groundwater maps help people in many ways. A map can show where harmful chemicals would go if they were spilled on the surface of the ground. People look at groundwater maps to figure out why wells are

Farmers in the southwestern United States pump groundwater to water their crops.

low or dry. A map also can show what would happen to groundwater if people dammed a river.

Studying the Past

Beach studies how ancient civilizations used groundwater. She travels to the sites of ancient cities in Mexico, Belize, Turkey, Syria, and other countries. Beach looks at ancient wells and water systems. She tries to learn if wells might have dried up. Or she might find that unsafe water harmed ancient people. Her research helps archaeologists learn how ancient people lived. Archaeologists are scientists who dig up and study objects to learn about the past.

Beach creates historical groundwater maps based on her research. These maps show where groundwater in a certain place flowed at different times in history. These maps help scientists see how water levels have changed over time. Beach's research may help people learn how groundwater should best be used in the future.

Sheryl Luzzadder Beach conducts groundwater research in Belize.

Chapter 3

Sandra Corso

Sandra Corso grew up in Brazil. She was always curious about the world around her. She asked many questions.

Corso went to college in the United States. She studied oceanography. Oceanographers study the ocean. Corso also studied marine biology. This science focuses on plants and animals in the ocean. Corso earned a bachelor's degree from the University of Washington in Seattle, Washington.

Today, she works in the geophysics department at the University of Washington as a seismic analyst. She studies earthquakes.

Sandra Corso studies earthquakes.

Sandra Corso visits seismic stations in the mountains of Washington and Oregon.

This sudden shaking of the ground happens when huge rock masses called plates shift. These plate shifts are very powerful.

Earthquakes can cause great damage. They can destroy buildings, bridges, and roads. They may open cracks in the ground or push up land to create cliffs. Earthquakes near or under the ocean can create tsunamis. A tsunami is a powerful wave that can cause damage when it reaches land.

Faults

Corso studies earthquake activity in Washington and Oregon. These states lie in a zone of faults. A fault is a crack in the earth's outer layer where two plates meet. The earth has split into many plates over millions of years. Washington and Oregon are in the fault zone where the Juan de Fuca plate and the North American plate meet. Earthquakes can happen when the plate edges move against each other.

Thousands of earthquakes happen each year under Washington and Oregon. But most of these earthquakes are small. People in the region notice only about 24 earthquakes each year. Corso and other scientists believe large earthquakes happen in Washington and Oregon about every 300 to 1,000 years.

Measuring Earthquakes

Seismic analysts like Corso use special tools called seismometers to measure earthquakes.

Seismometers measure earthquakes using the Richter magnitude scale. This scale grades the strength of an earthquake from one to 10. An earthquake that people hardly feel would measure about two on the scale. Powerful earthquakes might measure more than eight.

Corso tracks the location and strength of earthquakes through readings from seismic stations. More than 130 stations measure earthquakes in the Washington and Oregon area. The stations send information to computers at Washington State University in Pullman, Washington. Corso checks the readings and stores them in a computer system. She then creates maps showing where the earthquakes happened.

Part of Corso's job is to check equipment at stations in the Cascade Mountains. She tests the seismometers to make sure they work. She also tests the strength of signals sent out from the stations' radios. The stations receive alarm signals if an earthquake happens nearby. The signals also are sent to computers at the

Sandra Corso checks an electrical system at a seismic station.

university. Corso can collect information about the earthquake from wherever she is working.

Corso shares her findings with scientists around the world. Her work helps scientists learn more about earthquakes. Scientists use Corso's findings to understand how underground pressure builds up on a fault. These facts may help scientists predict when an earthquake will happen. These predictions may save lives.

Chapter 4

Jami Girard

Jami Girard liked to play in dirt when she was growing up in Anaconda, Montana. Today, she works with dirt and rocks. Girard is a mining engineer. She makes plans for building mines.

Girard attended the Montana College of Mineral Science and Technology in Butte, Montana. She earned a bachelor's degree in computer programming and mining engineering. Today, she works for the National Institute for Occupational Safety and Health in Spokane, Washington. Girard tries to find ways to make mines and mining tools safer.

Jami Girard is a mining engineer. She studies the earth to make plans for building mines.

Mining

People use metals and other minerals to make common items such as cars, tools, and wire. Even toothpaste and soda pop have minerals in them. Some minerals such as gold and diamonds are worth large amounts of money.

Girard works with geologists. Geologists who work for mining companies search for mineral deposits in the ground. Deposits are large amounts of minerals. Some deposits are near the surface. Others dip down deep into the ground. These deep deposits are called veins.

Mining engineers like Girard find the best ways to dig minerals out of the ground. Miners dig open-pit mines for surface deposits. They use machines to scrape rock from the land. Miners then separate the minerals from the rock. Miners build underground mines to reach veins.

People must work hard to build an underground mine. Miners first dig vertical holes called shafts into the ground. They then

Girard uses a tractor to remove dirt and rocks from a mine tunnel.

EERE
STAR

Jami Girard works to make the bolting process safer in mines. Miners use bolts to hold up the roofs of mines.

make tunnels sideways into the rock to reach the veins. To make the tunnels, miners first drill holes into the rock. They place explosives in the holes. Explosives blast the rock. Small tractors with front-end loaders remove blasted rock from the tunnel.

Robots

Girard and other mining engineers know that building an underground tunnel is risky. The roofs of tunnels sometimes crack and fall. Miners use bolts to hold up the roofs. But loose pieces can fall from the roofs. These falling rocks hurt hundreds of miners each year.

Girard is making plans for a robot that can put the bolts in place. The robot looks like a short tractor. It has wheels and many arms that can drill holes in the rock. The robot squirts a mix that is like glue into the holes. Then it puts the bolts tightly into the holes. Girard controls the robot with a computer at a safe distance from the tunnel. Girard's research may make rock bolting safer and easier.

PennState

Chapter 5

Kelley Anne Gittis

Kelley Anne Gittis was born in Canada. She grew up in Sydney, Nova Scotia. She earned a bachelor's degree in geology from St. Francis Xavier University in Antigonish, Nova Scotia.

Today, Gittis is a paleontologist. She works for the Academy of Natural Sciences in Philadelphia. She finds and studies fossils. Gittis travels to fossil sites in the United States and Canada. She digs up fossils such as dinosaur bones and plant imprints.

Digs

Scientists search for ancient remains at digs. Gittis works with a team to divide a site into

Kelley Anne Gittis is a paleontologist. She finds and studies fossils.

sections and make a site map. The team carefully records what they find in each section.

Scientists use tools of all sizes during digs. Large axes and shovels help break up thick rock. Tiny brushes help clear dirt from fossils. Scientists must be careful not to damage fossils as they work.

Gittis has learned that all the findings at a site are important. For example, fossils found around the bones of a dinosaur tell scientists a great deal about the dinosaur. Scientists might find plant or animal fossils that indicate what the dinosaur ate.

Scientists study the rock around the bones to find out when the dinosaur lived. Other fossils might show what the climate was like at that time. All of these clues may help Gittis and other scientists learn how dinosaurs lived and why they died.

Mastodon Dig

One of Gittis' most important digs was at an open-pit mine in Nova Scotia. Miners had found the remains of a mastodon there.

Kelley Anne Gittis looks at the skull of a Tyrannosaurus rex.

Mastodons were animals that looked like giant elephants. Paleontologists from the Nova Scotia Museum of Natural History asked Gittis to help with the dig.

The position of the remains caused some problems. The mastodon remains were in clay soil. Parts of the mastodon bones stuck out from the side of the mine. Rain began to fall shortly after Gittis and her team arrived at the site.

The rain made the clay around the mastodon crack. The mastodon could have slid into the mine if the clay had become too wet. So Gittis and the other scientists built a shelter over the site to keep it dry.

The dig was hard. The scientists worked for nine months in all kinds of weather. But their efforts resulted in important findings. They discovered many other ancient animal fossils on the same site as the mastodon. The fossils included ancient turtles, fish, birds, frogs, and beavers. These findings indicated the kinds of animals that lived in the area 80,000 years ago.

The bones Gittis and the other scientists found were wet and weak. The scientists had to carefully carve the clay away from the bones. Gittis forced a mixture of glue into the bones to make them stronger. Scientists then moved the bones to the Nova Scotia Museum of Natural History.

The scientists took many steps to make sure the bones arrived safely at the museum. They first wrapped the bones in paper towels. They

Kelley Anne Gittis digs up fossils such as this dinosaur thighbone.

Penn State

then ripped a coarse material called burlap into strips. The scientists dipped the burlap strips in wet plaster and layered them on the bones. They let the plaster dry to form casts. These casts were like those a doctor would put on a broken arm.

Gittis and other scientists have begun to clean and study all the bones they found. This work could take years. But the scientists may learn what the animals were like when they were alive. The bones also could help scientists better understand animals that are alive today. Scientists may discover how certain animals have changed over time.

Kelley Anne Gittis uses plaster and strips of burlap to make a protective cast around a fossil.

Chapter 6

Patricia Rogers

Patricia Rogers had two high school teachers who encouraged her interest in science. She continued to study science in college. Rogers earned a bachelor's degree in geological sciences from Harvard University in Cambridge, Massachusetts. She also holds a master's degree in geology and a doctorate in geophysics from Johns Hopkins University in Baltimore, Maryland.

Today, Rogers is a scientist at the National Aeronautics and Space Administration (NASA) headquarters in Washington, D.C. NASA is a government agency that directs space exploration for the United States.

Patricia Rogers is a scientist at the National Aeronautics and Space Administration.

Patricia Rogers studies volcanoes on Mars.

Studying Mars

Rogers has a special interest in Mars. Mars is a cold planet that cannot support life. Some scientists believe Mars once looked like Earth. Mars has many of the same elements found on ice caps on Earth. Frozen water may exist underground on Mars. Like Earth, Mars also has minerals. The air on Mars is mostly carbon dioxide. This gas also exists in air on Earth.

Scientists have studied meteorites on Earth that they believe came from Mars. This matter fell from space to Earth. The meteorite has small objects in it that may be fossils of tiny creatures. Some scientists believe the creatures lived on Mars and died out when the climate on Mars changed. The air became cold and rivers disappeared. Some scientists think Earth's climate also could experience major changes sometime in the future.

Rogers studies volcanoes on Mars and other planets. The volcanoes on Mars have not been active for millions of years. But the fact that they exist is important to scientists. The presence of volcanoes is one reason that scientists think Mars was once like Earth. Rogers' findings may help scientists learn more about volcanoes on Earth.

Missions to Mars

Rogers manages two special projects at NASA. She works on the Mars Global Surveyor mission and on the Mars 2001 mission. These missions are part of NASA's long-term exploration of Mars.

The Mars Global Surveyor mission sent a spacecraft to Mars in November 1996. The flight from Earth to Mars took 10 months. The Mars Global Surveyor will orbit Mars for about two years. The purpose of the mission is to map the whole planet. The maps will include the volcanoes that Rogers studies. The Surveyor will send detailed pictures of the volcanoes and other land features back to Earth. Rogers and other scientists will study the Surveyor's findings.

Rogers also manages the Mars 2001 mission. This mission will send a type of robot called a rover to the surface of Mars. The rover will collect rock samples. Scientists will study the rock samples to learn more about the geologic makeup of Mars.

The Mars 2001 mission also will help scientists find ways for people to land safely on Mars. Scientists want to make sure people will not be hurt by gases in the air. Scientists also want to develop fuels that will send spacecraft safely through the atmosphere of Mars. This will make sure that people who go to Mars can come back to Earth.

Scientists work on part of the Mars Global Surveyor spacecraft.

Words to Know

dig (DIG)—the process of searching for ancient remains

fault (FAWLT)—a crack in the earth where two plates meet

geology (jee-AHL-uh-jee)—the study of minerals, rocks, and soil

geophysics (jee-oh-FIH-zihks)—the study of Earth using the principles of physics

hydrology (hy-DRAH-luh-jee)—the study of water

marine biology (muh-REEN bye-AH-luh-jee)—the study of plants and animals in the ocean

oceanography (oh-shuh-NAH-gra-fee)—the study of the ocean

paleontologist (pay-lee-uhn-TAH-luh-jihst)—a scientist who finds and studies fossils

To Learn More

Allen, Carol. *Earth: All about Earthquakes, Volcanoes, Glaciers, Oceans, and More.* Toronto: Owl Communications, 1993.

Bramwell, Martyn. *Volcanoes and Earthquakes.* Earth Science Library. New York: Franklin Watts, 1994.

Gibbons, Gail. *Planet Earth, Inside Out.* New York: Morrow Junior Books, 1995.

Hooper, Meredith. *The Pebble in My Pocket: A History of Our Earth.* New York: Viking Children's Books, 1996.

Kipp, Steven L. *Earth.* The Galaxy. Mankato, Minn.: Bridgestone Books, 1998.

Pinet, Michele. *Be Your Own Rock and Mineral Expert.* New York: Sterling Publishing, 1997.

Sattler, Helen Roney. *Our Patchwork Planet: The Story of Plate Tectonics.* New York: Lothrop, Lee & Shepard Books, 1995.

Useful Addresses

American Geological Institute
4220 King Street
Alexandria, VA 22302-1502

Association for Women in Science
1200 New York Avenue NW
Suite 650
Washington, DC 20005

Geological Association of Canada
Department of Earth Sciences
Memorial University of Newfoundland
St. John's, NF A1B 3X5
Canada

Geological Society of America
P.O. Box 9140
Boulder, CO 80301

Geological Survey of Canada
601 Booth Street
Ottawa, ON K1A 0E8
Canada

Internet Sites

Ask a Geologist
http://walrus.wr.usgs.gov/docs/ask-a-ge.html

Hydrology Primer
http://wwwdmorll.er.usgs.gov/~bjsmith/outreach/hydrology.primer.html

Minerals and Metals at Home!
http://www.nrcan.gc.ca/mms/wealth/intro-e.htm

Some Career Paths in the Geosciences
http://www.science.uwaterloo.ca/earth/geoscience/jobs.html#jobs

Space Gateway—Mars Discoveries
http://www.sci.fi/~iscsi/marsdiscoveries.html

Volcano World
http://volcano.und.nodak.edu

Index